LET'S ROCK!

What Are Fossils?

Natalie Hyde

Crabtree Publishing Company

www.crabtreebooks.com

Crabtree Publishing Company

www.crabtreebooks.com

Author: Natalie Hyde
Publishing plan research and development:
  Sean Charlebois, Reagan Miller
  Crabtree Publishing Company
Project coordinator: Kathy Middleton
Photo research: Tibor Choleva, Melissa McClellan
Design: Tibor Choleva
Editor: Adrianna Morganelli
Proofreaders: Rachel Stuckey, Crystal Sikkens
Production coordinator: Margaret Amy Salter
Prepress technician: Margaret Amy Salter
Print coordinator: Katherine Berti

Geological consultant:
Dr. Kevin Seymour, Royal Ontario Museum

Cover: Dinosaur fossil (center); fossilized fern
(bottom right); shell fossils (left); ancient fossil
(bottom middle)

Title page: A Replica of saber tooth tiger skull
embedded in rock

This book was produced for Crabtree Publishing
Company by BlueAppleWorks.

Photographs and reproductions:
© dreamstime.com: Buradaki(headline and boxtop image),Eti Swinford(title page, 19
right), Dmitry Ersler(4/5 large),Steve Estvanik(6 left), AleZanIT(7 bottom),Mr1805(10/11
large), Michael James(12/13 large),Petrina Calabalic(14 left),Maksims Osipovs(14
bottom),Petr Pokorny (15 right), Kuzmichevdmitry(19 bottom left),Tihis (20 bottom
left),Goran Bogicevic(23 top),Onepony(24/25 bottom),Andrey Troitskiy(24/25
large),Martinzak (25 left),Natalia Pavlova(25 right),Gunold Brunbauer(26/27
large),Lynx3118(27 bottom left),Marcio Silva (27 bottom right), Feng Hui (28/29 large),(28
top) / © fotolia: chungking(21 top left) / © iStockphoto.com: Arpad Benedek(6 top),
Michael Gray(8 right), Klaus Nilkens(10) / © Shutterstock.com: Michael C. Gray (cover:
center), Falk Kienas (cover: bottom right), Triff (bottom middle), AleZanIT (left), Kaarsten
(headline image), Falk Kienas(background image), DM7(4/5 dinsoaur),Anetlanda (5
middle), ronstik(5 bottom),Lorraine Swanson(6 bottom),vichie81(7 top),Tim Burrett(8
bottom left),Alena Hovorkova(8 bottom),MarcelClemens(9 top), Alena Hovorkova (9
bottom),Mike Brake(12 top),Juriah Mosin(12 bottom),bestimagesevercom(13 middle), Roy
Palmer(14 top right),Galyna Andrushko(14 middle),NitroCephal(14/15 large), Falk Kienas
(15 top), Andrey Pavlov(15 bottom), Antonio Abrignani (16 top),Bryan Busovicki(16/17
large),Alex James Bramwell (19 top left), Aleksandar Todorovic(19 bottom right),Tom
Grundy(20 top), Michal Baranski(21 top right),robert paul van beets(21 bottom left),Bill
Florence(21 bottom right),Andreas Meyer(24 bottom left),topal(27 top),Jaroslaw
Grudzinski(28 bottom) / ©Thinkstock: Hemera(7 middle), iStockphoto(13
left),Comstock(20/21 large), Hemera Technologies/Getty Images(27 middle right),
iStockphoto(29 top), Getty Images (29 bottom) / Science Photo Library: Philippe
Plailly/Eurelios (17 top),Volker Steger(26 bottom) / © Ellen McKnight(7 bottom right)
Photographer's Direct: © Robert Kawka(11 top) / © Mark Buford(11 middle) / Public
domain (5 middle, 11 bottom, 18, 20 right, National Science Foundation 22 bottom, 23
middle right, 24 middle) / © A. Ochsenreiter, courtesy of South Tyrol Museum of
Archaeology (17 bottom 3 images) / © Carlyn Iverson, Absolute Science Illustration: 13
bottom, 22 top, 23 left, 23 bottom right / © David Brock illustrations: 4

Library and Archives Canada Cataloguing in Publication

Hyde, Natalie, 1963-
    What are fossils? / Natalie Hyde.

(Let's rock)
Includes index.
Issued also in electronic formats.
ISBN 978-0-7787-7214-9 (bound).--ISBN 978-0-7787-7219-4 (pbk.)

    1. Fossils--Juvenile literature. I. Title. II. Series: Let's rock
(St. Catharines, Ont.)

QE714.5.H93 2012   j560   C2012-900250-X

Library of Congress Cataloging-in-Publication Data

CIP available at Library of Congress

Crabtree Publishing Company

www.crabtreebooks.com   1-800-387-7650

Printed in Canada/022012/AV20120110

Published in Canada
Crabtree Publishing
616 Welland Ave.
St. Catharines, Ontario
L2M 5V6

Published in the United States
Crabtree Publishing
PMB 59051
350 Fifth Avenue, 59th Floor
New York, New York 10118

Published in the United Kingdom
Crabtree Publishing
Maritime House
Basin Road North, Hove
BN41 1WR

Published in Australia
Crabtree Publishing
3 Charles Street
Coburg North
VIC 3058

CONTENTS

Once Upon a Time   4

The Raiders of the Past   6

Stay in Shape   8

Traces in Stone   10

Ancient Bones   12

Golden Traps   14

Frozen Section   16

That Sinking Feeling   18

Rock Gardens   20

Unusual Animals   22

Not Dragons   24

Great...Great...Grandparents   26

Bone Hunting   28

Glossary   30

More Information   31

Index   32

ONCE UPON A TIME

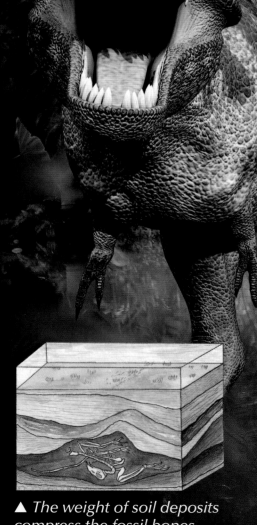

The plants and animals that lived on Earth millions of years ago are very different from the ones that live today. How do we know what kind of creatures roamed the planet so long ago? We find traces of them in fossils.

PRESERVED FROM THE PAST

The remains or traces of living organisms that have been preserved are called fossils. Most plants and animals **decompose** quickly after death. Bacteria are responsible for breaking down organisms. Sometimes certain materials stop or delay decomposition. When this happens, fossils can form.

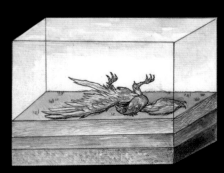

▲ An animal dies and their tissue starts to decompose.

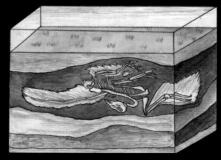

▲ Layers of sediment cover the bones.

▲ The weight of soil deposits compress the fossil bones.

BURGESS SHALE

✳ The Burgess Shale in Yoho National Park in British Columbia, Canada, is one of the most important fossil beds in the world. Millions of years ago, the area was flat and covered by a warm shallow sea. When sea creatures died they were buried under mud. The heat and pressure from the layers of sediment turned the mud into shale and the sea creatures into fossils. Later, the seabed was pushed upward during mountain building. Now this fossil bed is high up in the Rocky Mountains.

FORMING METHODS

Different types of fossils are formed in different ways. Sometimes a plant or animal is buried under layers of mud or clay. Over time these layers are pressed together to form **sedimentary rock** that keeps the shapes of these organisms. Other times minerals in water seep into the organism's remains and harden. This creates a **mineralized** copy of the organism.

BACTERIA-FREE

Plants and animals sometimes get trapped in material that stops bacteria from doing their job of breaking down tissue. Bog water, tar, **resin**, ice, and volcanic ash can cover plants and animals and preserve them.

▼ Burgess Shale was once at the bottom of a shallow sea.

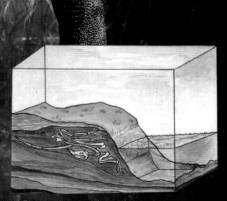

▲ The erosion process exposes the fossil.

▼ Many ancient creatures are found in **prehistoric** tree resin called amber.

5

THE RAIDERS OF THE PAST

Paleontologists are scientists who study fossils to learn about life on our planet long ago. Fossils are the only way we can know about the types of plants and animals that lived on Earth before human beings. Fossils help us understand how and where life began and how it has changed over time.

DATING FOSSILS

Paleontologists can date fossils by determining the age of the rocks nearby. Tiny particles in rocks such as carbon or uranium, break down, or decay at a certain rate. By measuring how much of the element remains, scientists can pinpoint the age of the rock.

▲ *This paleontologist is examining a fossil embedded in a rock.*

▼ *The sedimentary rock layers in the Alberta **Badlands**, in Canada, are full of fossils.*

▼ *Fossils of the* Albertosaurus *are found only in Alberta, Canada. The name of this dinosaur means "Lizard from Alberta."*

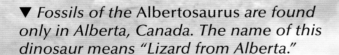

WHERE DID THEY GO?

✳ Trilobites were sea creatures that disappeared about 250 million years ago. Fossils have pointed to times in Earth's history when a huge number of plants and animals died off suddenly. These **mass extinctions** may have been caused by volcanic activity, climate change, or impacts from asteroids.

▼ *Trilobites are excellent index fossils.*

OLD AND YOUNG

The oldest fossils we've found so far are of ancient stromatolites. Stromatolites are rock columns formed by the buildup of minerals around the growth of algae. While the oldest fossil stromatolites date back almost three billion years ago, new stromatolites are still forming in coastal waters today.

▶ *Modern stromatolites in coastal waters of Australia*

LINED UP IN TIME

Fossils found in different ages of rocks give scientists a good timeline of when species of animals and plants **evolved** or went extinct. Some fossils or groups of fossils may have lived for only a few hundred thousand years— a short time in Earth's history. When paleontologists find these fossils, known as index fossils, they can date the layer of rock. Index fossils help to place new fossils on the timeline.

▼ *Ammonite fossils give us good clues of how the species looked before it went extinct.*

STAY IN SHAPE

When a plant or an animal is covered with mud or clay, an **imprint** fossil is created. These fossils often have very precise details that tell paleontologists what the plant or animal might have looked like.

FOLDS IN MOLDS

After an organism is pressed into mud or clay, it may completely **disintegrate** over time and leave only an imprint behind. This is called a mold. Molds are an image of the outside of an organism. Fossil molds of ancient seashells show even the smallest folds in their shells.

▼ *Well preserved details of a fossilized shell*

CASTS OF DOOM

✳ Some of the most famous molds and casts are from the ancient city of Pompeii, in Italy. In 79 AD, Mount Vesuvius **erupted** and quickly covered the Roman town of Pompeii with so much ash, that the people couldn't escape. In modern times, archaeologists discovered large molds of the victims under the ash. Casts were created by filling these molds with plaster.

▼ *Casts preserve the last moments of the people of Pompeii.*

MAKE YOUR OWN FOSSIL

You will need:

- a paper plate
- a paper cup
- modeling clay
- an object to cast: seashell, small plastic figurine
- petroleum jelly
- plaster of Paris
- a plastic spoon

Place a piece of clay about the size of a tennis ball on the plate. Cover the object to cast with a thin layer of petroleum jelly. Press the object into the clay. Carefully remove the object so a clear imprint remains in the clay. You have just made a mold! Mix four spoons of plaster of Paris with two spoons of water in the paper cup. Pour the plaster mixture into the mold. Allow the plaster to harden for about 15 to 20 minutes. Separate the clay from the plaster.

The plaster is now a cast of your object!

ROCK SOLID COPIES

Sometimes minerals in the water seep into a mold and fill it up. This creates a copy of the plant or animal made of rock. This is called a cast. Casts are a wonderful way to see the full shape and size of the original organism.

▼ *Fossil casts and imprints of **marine** organisms give scientists a good idea of prehistoric life in oceans.*

TRACES IN STONE

Trace fossils preserve an organism's activity. Imprints of nests, trails, footprints, as well as fossilized poop are all considered trace fossils.

DAILY ROUTINES

Molds and casts are created after an organism has died, but trace fossils show direct evidence of what a creature did in its daily life. These fossils give scientists valuable information about the habits of extinct creatures. Did they crawl, creep, or hop? Was their home a nest, burrow, or tunnel?

▼ *Fossilized footprints can give paleontologists clues about the size of dinosaurs.*

FAST AND SLOW

Fossilized footprints can show how fast or slow the creature moved, depending on how far apart the tracks are. The depths of the prints also tell us how much an animal might have weighed.

▶ Plateosaurus *leaving footprints in prehistoric mud*

GOING NUMBER TWO

Coprolites are fossilized poop. These fossils give paleontologists information on the diet of ancient creatures. Coprolites can also provide information on plant species. **Parasite** remains in coprolites can also tell scientists about ancient diseases.

▲ *By examining coprolites, paleontologists are able to find information about the diet of the animal.*

STOMACH STONES

✳ Gastroliths are rocks swallowed by animals to help grind food in their stomachs. They are smoothed and polished by bumping into the other stones while the creature digests its food, like in a rock tumbler. Fossil gastroliths found near dinosaur remains can weigh several pounds.

▼ *Fossilized gastroliths look like pebbles.*

TINY BURROWS

Some fossil burrows are over one billion years old. These little holes in rocks were once the hiding places of tiny sea creatures. There are no imprint fossils for these animals, so the trace fossils are the only clue that they once lived.

▶ *Burrows are a type of trace fossil often found in sedimentary rocks.*

ANCIENT BONES

Paleontologists call fossils that were once part of a plant or animal's structure, body fossils. Most body fossils are from the hard parts of an animal like bones, teeth, and claws.

BETTER CHANCES
Creatures that had a hard outer shell, like trilobites, or a tough skeleton, like dinosaurs, had a better chance of becoming a fossil than creatures with mostly soft tissue, like jellyfish or worms.

▲ Well preserved fossil of an ancient turtle

▼ Reconstruction of a dinosaur's nest

CAREFUL WITH THE EGGS!
Over 200 egg fossil sites have been found around the world. Paleontologists have discovered many things about dinosaurs by studying nest sites. Dinosaurs laid two to 20 eggs at a time. Most dinosaurs were too heavy to sit on a **clutch** of eggs without crushing them so they probably covered the nests with rotting plants to provide heat. Eggs found intact with **embryos** inside have given scientists important information about how dinosaurs developed.

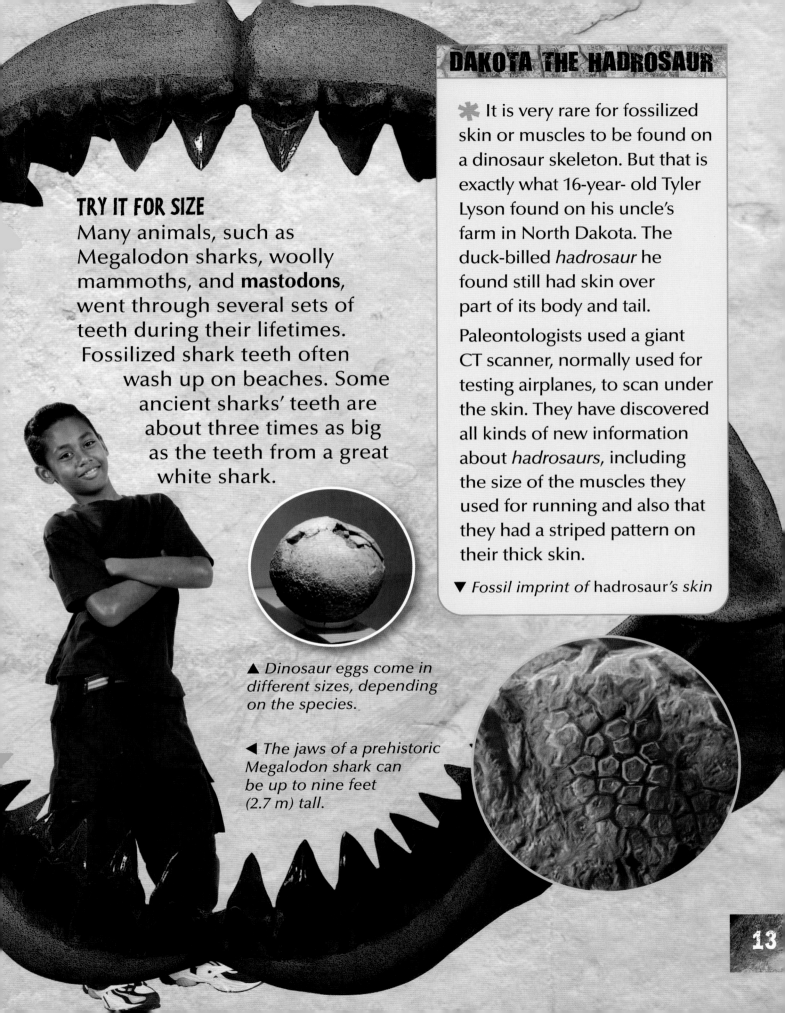

TRY IT FOR SIZE

Many animals, such as Megalodon sharks, woolly mammoths, and **mastodons**, went through several sets of teeth during their lifetimes. Fossilized shark teeth often wash up on beaches. Some ancient sharks' teeth are about three times as big as the teeth from a great white shark.

▲ Dinosaur eggs come in different sizes, depending on the species.

◄ The jaws of a prehistoric Megalodon shark can be up to nine feet (2.7 m) tall.

DAKOTA THE HADROSAUR

✳ It is very rare for fossilized skin or muscles to be found on a dinosaur skeleton. But that is exactly what 16-year-old Tyler Lyson found on his uncle's farm in North Dakota. The duck-billed *hadrosaur* he found still had skin over part of its body and tail.

Paleontologists used a giant CT scanner, normally used for testing airplanes, to scan under the skin. They have discovered all kinds of new information about *hadrosaurs*, including the size of the muscles they used for running and also that they had a striped pattern on their thick skin.

▼ *Fossil imprint of* hadrosaur's skin

GOLDEN TRAPS

It was an unlucky day in the life of insects and even tiny lizards millions of years ago when they got stuck in tree resin. Unlucky for them, but lucky for us. The tiny creatures and plants captured in fossilized resin, called amber, provide amazing information for scientists.

ALL INCLUSIVE

Plant and animal parts found in amber are called inclusions. These organisms were totally covered in resin so they did not decay. Ancient plants and animals are preserved exactly as they appeared before humans even existed. Scientists have learned many things from inclusions. For example, ancient mosquitoes had mouths strong enough to pierce the thick skin of dinosaurs.

TIME STOP

Scientists have found more than 1,000 extinct species of insects in amber. Some of these include a prehistoric fly caught in the middle of laying eggs, a group of ants working together to eat a millipede, stingless bees, and even grasshoppers.

▲ *A grasshopper trapped in ancient amber*

▲ *Even frogs were trapped in amber.*

◄ *Pieces of unpolished amber washed up on a beach.*

MAKE YOUR OWN AMBER FOSSIL!

You will need:

- a dead insect (look on window ledges or spider webs), a seed, or a leaf
- plastic pop bottle cap
- clear nail polish
- food coloring (yellow and red)
- tweezers or needle-nose pliers
- newspapers

Place the pop bottle cap, empty side up on the newspapers. Using the tweezers, place your specimen into the empty cap. Place several drops of yellow food coloring in the nail polish. Add a drop of red to make a more amber color. Drip the polish over the specimen until it is covered and put aside to dry. Cut or break off the plastic bottle cap. You now have your own inclusion!

◄ *Perfectly preserved fly in an amber "time capsule."*

SNEAK PEEK

Other inclusions show scientists what the seeds, bark, buds, and leaves of prehistoric plants looked like. Pieces of mammal hair and feathers give us a peek at what extinct animals really looked like.

▼ *Pieces of plant material in ancient resin*

▼*Ants can get stuck in sap and appear thousands of years later in a piece of amber.*

FROZEN SECTION

Some of the biggest and most complete fossils on our planet have been found in Earth's deep freeze: **glaciers** and ice fields. Entire woolly mammoths, bison, and even humans have been found frozen in time.

WELL PRESERVED

Frozen organisms are not true fossils because they are not mineralized. They are preserved, however, and give paleontologists a lot of information that regular fossils cannot.

WATCH YOUR STEP!

Frozen plant and animal specimens were usually caught in flash floods or fell into **crevasses**. Covered quickly with water and then frozen, the plant and animal tissue did not have time to decay.

ICE MUMMIES

✳ The soft tissue in frozen fossils is a rich source of information. Sometimes it can even solve a mystery! Tissue samples from the ice mummies of three men from the 1845 Franklin Expedition to find the Northwest Passage, led scientists to the discovery that the men were being poisoned by lead tin cans from their food supply.

▲ *Franklin and his crew of 128 men died when their ships became stuck in ice in the Canadian Arctic.*

WOOLLY BABY

In 1977, the frozen remains of a baby woolly mammoth were discovered in Siberia. Scientists named him Dima. The seven-or eight-month-old had been dead for 40,000 years, but was so perfectly preserved that scientists could measure and weigh him. He looked just like a modern baby elephant, except he had fur and much smaller ears.

▲ Woolly mammoths were well adapted to the cold. Their shaggy hair was up to three feet (one m) in length.

HIKING IN THE PAST

In 1991, hikers in the Swiss Alps stumbled across the frozen body of a 5,300-year-old man! Known as Iceman, he was found with straw shoes, a gopher-skin coat, and a copper axe. Scientists were able to examine the contents of his stomach to learn that his last meal had been deer meat, bread, and fruit.

◄ A life-like reconstruction of Iceman is on display in the South Tyrol Museum of Archaeology in Bolzano, Italy.

▼ Iceman's shoes and hat

THAT SINKING FEELING

Bogs are areas where rotting plants, moss, and water combine to make spongy swampland. The water is very **acidic** and not friendly to the bacteria that break down organic matter. Organisms that died in a bog would have been preserved by the chemicals in the water and the lack of oxygen or bacteria.

WIDE ENOUGH?

Most bogs formed from meltwater after the last Ice Age. Most of the fossils found in bogs date from this time. Some amazing specimens have been preserved in bogs. The Irish elk was a giant deer over seven feet (two meters) tall with antlers as wide as a tank!

▼ *While most Irish elk skeletons have been found in Ireland, the deer also lived in other places.*

BOGGY CEMETERY

✱ Hundreds of perfectly preserved human remains, known as bog bodies, have been found in bogs throughout Northern Europe. Scientists believe most of them are from the Iron Age and may have been killed as a punishment or in a ritual sacrifice.

▼ *The Tollund Man is a naturally mummified bog body found in Denmark.*

STICKY PITS

Places where crude oil seeps out of the ground, also known as "tar pits," are another natural formation that can trap and preserve plants and animals. Crude oil is created from buried ancient sea life. When it reaches the surface it evaporates and changes into dark brown to black sticky tar called **asphalt**.

▼ *If an animal falls into a tar pit it is unlikely to escape from the sticky asphalt.*

WHAT A BAD PLACE TO EAT!

In the heat of summer the tops of tar pits can harden. Blowing dust and leaves can then hide the pits from view. Ancient animals would walk onto the pits and stick to the tar like flies on flypaper. **Predators** would find an easy snack, but could also become stuck in the tar.

▼ *Fossil of a saber-toothed cat in a tar pit*

THE LA BREA TAR PITS

✳ The Rancho La Brea in Los Angeles is one of the best known asphalt seeps or tar pits. Scientists have found the remains of a wide variety of organisms including scorpions, mammoths, saber-toothed cats, and camels.

◄ *Saber-toothed cats were fierce hunters.*

ROCK GARDENS

Plant fossils have given paleobotanists, or people who study plant fossils, much information about the environment on Earth millions of years ago. Many plants have changed very little from their ancient **ancestors**. Other species of plants have disappeared completely.

WAY TO GO, GINKGO!

Most plant fossils are only a piece of a plant: a leaf, a piece of bark, a flower, or a seed. Because most plants quickly decompose, it is rare to have an imprint of the entire organism. Casts of modern day looking leaves of maple, poplar, willow, and oak have been found. Fossilized leaves of ginkgo plants are so similar to today's plant that the ginkgo is considered a living fossil.

▲ *Plant fossils mostly show small, incomplete pieces of ancient plants.*

▶ *This fossil of a ginkgo leaf looks exactly like the present day ginkgo leaves.*

FERNS IN THEIR BILLIONS

Ferns are the most common plant fossil, and the oldest is from 360 million years ago. At that time, forests and swamps were covered by billions of seed ferns. Scientists believe that layers and layers of dead ferns buried in peat bogs and pressed together created the large coal **deposits** in Pennsylvania and West Virginia.

▼ Fern fossils are very common in coal mining areas.

ICE FOREST!

✳ High in the Arctic, on Canada's Axel Heiberg Island, researchers stumbled upon a mummified forest! The trees on this barren, frozen island grew when the landmass was much farther south and temperatures were higher. After the continents moved north, the dry, cold air preserved the fallen trees. Millions of years later, the wood can be cut and burned.

▶ Fossil of scale-shaped tree bark

DIAMOND BARK

Some fossils show paleobotanists a very alien-looking world. Ancient trees had unusual bark patterns. Some tree barks had diamond-shaped patterns and others looked like fish scales.

STONE FOREST!

Sometimes trees or even entire forests fell and were covered by mud and clay. Over a long period of time, minerals seeped into the structure of the wood and created rock. Mineralized wood is called "petrified" and can be many colors depending on the different minerals in the wood.

◀ The term "petrified" comes from the Greek language. It means "turned into stone."

UNUSUAL ANIMALS

There are literally millions of different animal fossils. They range from tiny marine creatures to the towering *tyrannosaur*. But scientists believe that 99 percent of all creatures that ever existed haven't left a fossil record. We can only imagine how many different kinds of animals have called Earth their home.

▼ *Tiktaalik lived approximately 375 million years ago. Scientists think that the creature had primitive lungs as well as gills. This would have been useful in shallow water.*

FISH THAT COULD DO PUSH-UPS!

✳ In 2004, paleontologists working in Canada's Nunavut Territory discovered the fossil of a fish that had limb-like fins. The shape of the bones in its front fins allowed Tiktaalik to prop its body up in a push-up position. Tiktaalik is considered one of the missing links between fish and land animals.

▼ *Tiktaalik was named by Inuit elders of Nunavut, where the fossil was discovered.*

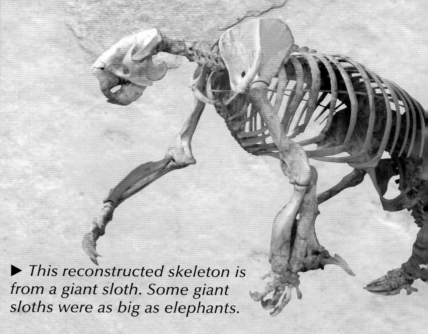

RAREST ANIMAL FOSSIL

Because octopuses are mostly made up of soft tissue that decomposes quickly, octopus fossils are the rarest and unlikeliest fossils. Scientists in Lebanon were thrilled to find five specimens that even had traces of ink.

▶ *This reconstructed skeleton is from a giant sloth. Some giant sloths were as big as elephants.*

▼ *Five well-preserved octopus fossils were found in 95-million year-old rocks in Lebanon.*

BIG AND TALL

Fossils of many ancient animals seem to be giant versions of modern animals: an ant as big as a small bird, a giant sloth, and the massive meat-eating kangaroo. Some paleontologists believe the high level of oxygen in the air helped creatures grow to enormous sizes.

WHAT A SHRIMP!

Strange and almost unbelievable animal fossils have been discovered in the Burgess Shale fossil site in British Columbia. One known as the "Unusual Shrimp" was a three-foot (one m) long creature that may have moved by its rippling flaps and attacked its **prey** with a ring of teeth. Another fossil looked like a centipede with five eyes and a long trunk that acted like a vacuum.

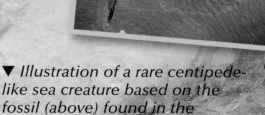

▼ *Illustration of a rare centipede-like sea creature based on the fossil (above) found in the Burgess Shale.*

NOT DRAGONS

The first people to dig up dinosaur fossils thought they were the bones of giants or dragons. In 1677, a scientist recognized that the fossil bone he had found belonged to a huge animal that had never been seen before.

BAD TO THE BONE

More complete dinosaur skeletons have been found in the Badlands of Alberta than at any other fossil site. Paleontologists believe that most of these dinosaurs were caught in flash floods that quickly covered them with sediment.

BITS AND PIECES

While scientists love to find complete dinosaurs, most of the time they only find bits and pieces of them. Each bone gives us important information about the ancient creatures. Skulls and teeth can identify the diet of the dinosaur. Backward curving teeth identify a meat eater who needed to hold on to a wriggling prey.

▶ The plant-eating Camarasaurus had flat teeth shaped like chisels.

DINOSAURS IN THE AIR

Most paleontologists believe that birds evolved from dinosaurs. Soft tissue and bone examinations from a fossilized *Tyrannosaurus rex* showed that dinosaurs and birds shared many features such as hollow bones and stomach stones.

▼ *Fossil of an ancient bird called* Archaeopteryx

BONES EVERYWHERE

✳ Dinosaur bones have been found on every **continent** on Earth including Antarctica in 1986.

COUNT YOUR TOES

The number of toes and fingers on a skeleton help identify different families of dinosaurs: some had three, some four, and others five. The length of the tibia, or lower leg bone, gives clues to the overall size of the animal. The larger the bone, the more weight it could carry.

▶ *Fossilized toes of dinosaurs*

◀ Tyrannosaurus rex *was one of the largest meat-eating land dinosaurs of all time.*

▼ *The Badlands in Alberta, Canada, contain many unique fossils.*

GREAT...GREAT...GRANDPARENTS

Fossils haven't just helped us understand ancient plants and animals, they have also helped us understand our human past.

SKULLS, BONES, AND SKELETONS

Scientists are using modern equipment to try to piece together the story of human evolution. Skulls, bones, and skeletons show that early man looked very different from modern *Homo sapiens*. By finding new ways to accurately date the fossils, scientists are building a fascinating timeline of change.

OUT OF AFRICA

Some of the earliest bones of human ancestors have been found in Africa and are up to six million years old. These early fossils show differences in appearance and abilities.

▶ Scientists look at the size of the skull to figure out how large a brain would have been. Larger brains mean a higher level of thinking.

SUPERVOLCANO

✳ Scientists believe that the **volcanic winter** caused by the eruption of the Toba supervolcano in Indonesia 70,000 years ago, may have caused the extinction of all species of early humans except *Homo sapiens*.

▶ A site where scientists look for prehistoric remains is call an excavation site.

COARSE VOICES

Paleontologists also look for the tiny **hyoid bones** from the throat area of human fossils. These bones are necessary for us to make the many different sounds for speech. By examining hip and pelvis bones, paleontologists can determine if the species walked upright or climbed trees.

▼ *The position of the pelvis bone in a skeleton shows how the animal would have moved.*

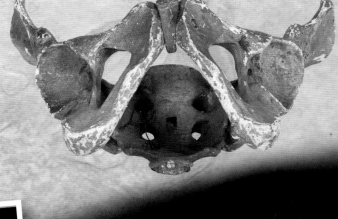

▲ *A paleontologist excavating a buried skeleton*

▼ *Skeletal remains of early humans can give scientists important information about human evolution.*

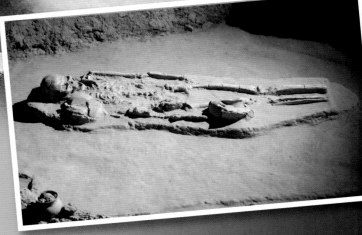

▶ *Scientists have enough information to reconstruct what early humans looked like.*

BONE HUNTING

Fossil collecting is a way to hold the past in your hands. As a hobby or as a career, fossil collecting is a fascinating look at our world and how it has changed.

STAY BY THE WATER

Fossils can be found in many places. The beach is a great place for fossil hunting because fossils can be washed up from other locations. Water can move fossils down streams and creeks, too. Rain can reveal fossils covered by soil.

SANDSTONE TREASURES

Sedimentary rock is the only type of rock that produces fossils, so limestone or sandstone **outcroppings** are good places to hunt for fossils. Fossils can be found in the cliffs or at the bottom where **debris** collects.

▲ *Fast-running creeks and streams can uncover fossils along their banks.*

▼ *The Jurassic Coast in England is a great place for fossil collecting. It covers 95 miles (153 km) of coastline from East Devon to Dorset.*

START YOUR OWN FOSSIL COLLECTION

You will need:

- rock hammer or small chisel hammer
- safety glasses
- plastic bags for specimens
- soft paper for wrapping specimens (tissue paper, facial tissues, etc.)
- fossil collecting handbook
- notebook and pen

Use the rock hammer to carefully separate layers of sedimentary rock. Write down the location and description of any fossils you find in your notebook. This information will help you identify the fossil later. Wrap fossils in soft paper and place them in plastic bags to carry them home. Label your fossils. Use an empty egg carton or a box with small sections to store your collection.

PLAY IT SAFE

Safety is an important part of fossil collecting. Collectors should get permission to go on private property, never go alone, and always wear clothing and safety equipment to protect them from cuts, scrapes, sunburn, and insects.

▲ These fossil collectors are looking at a stump of petrified wood.

▶ Statue of Hippocrates

AN OLD HOBBY!

✳ The Greek doctor, Hippocrates, was a fossil collector more than 2,000 years ago!

GLOSSARY

acidic Made up of materials that eat away at solids

ancestors Animals, plants, or humans from which others descended

asphalt A brownish-black sticky substance used for paving

Badlands An area of dry land eroded into deep ridges and peaks

clutch A set of eggs laid at one time

continent One of the main landmasses on Earth

crevasses A deep crack in the ground or ice

debris A buildup of rock fragments

decompose To rot or decay

deposit A buildup of material

disintegrate To break down into small parts

embryo An organism in the early stages of its development

erupted Exploded violently

evolved Developed or changed slowly over time

glacier A huge mass of ice traveling slowly over land

Homo sapiens The modern species of humans

hyoid bone A U-shaped bone at the base of the tongue needed for speech

imprint A mark made on a surface by pressure

marine Coming from the sea

mass extinction When many animal and plant species become extinct, or die off, at the same time

mastodon A large, extinct mammal similar to an elephant

mineralized Changed into mineral

outcroppings Parts of rock formations that are above the surface of the land

parasite An organism that lives off another organism

predators Animals that live by capturing and eating other animals

prehistoric Belonging to the time before recorded history

prey An animal who is hunted or caught for food

resin Sticky liquid produced by plants

sedimentary rock Rock formed by layers of sediment pressed together

volcanic winter A drop in Earth's temperature caused by volcanic ash blocking sunlight

MORE INFORMATION

FURTHER READING

Fossils: Clues to Ancient Life.
Arato, Rona. Crabtree Publishing, 2004.

Rocks and Fossils.
Pellant, Chris. Kingfisher, 2007.

Fossils.
Squire, Ann O. Children's Press, 2002.

WEBSITES

Fossils for Kids:
www.fossilsforkids.com

Fossils, facts and finds:
www.fossils-facts-and-finds.com

Science Kids: Bringing science and technology together:
http://www.sciencekids.co.nz/sciencefacts/earth/fossils.html

Dinosaur facts:
http://www.dinosaurfact.net/

INDEX

Albertosaurus 6
amber 5, 14-15
ammonite 7
Antarctica 25
archaeology 8
Archaeopteryx 25
asphalt 19
Axel Heiberg Island 21
bacteria 4
Badlands, Alberta 6, 24, 25
birds, relation to dinosaurs 25
bog bodies 18
bogs 18
Burgess Shale 5, 23
Camarasaurus 24
carbon dating 6
coal deposits 21
coprolites 11
decomposition 4, 6, 14, 16, 20, 23
Dima (woolly mammoth) 17
dinosaur eggs 12, 13
dinosaur nests 12
dragons 24
early humans 17, 27
evolution 7, 25, 26
extinction 7, 10, 15, 26
ferns 21
fossil bed 5
fossil cast 9
fossil collecting 28, 29

fossil molds 8
fossils,
    body 12-13
    burrow 11
    creation of 4
    frozen 16-17
    human 26
    imprint 8, 10, 11
    index 7
    mineralized 5, 16
    octopus 23
    trace 10-11
    unusual animal 22-23
Franklin Expedition 16
gastroliths 11
ginkgo 20
glaciers 16
hadrosaur 13
Hippocrates 29
Homo sapiens 26
Iceman 17
inclusions 14
insects 14
Jurassic Coast 28
kangaroo, meat-eating 23
Lyson, Tyler 13
mastodons 13
Megalodon sharks 13
Mount Vesuvius 8
Northwest Passage 16, 17
paleobotanists 20

paleontologists 6, 8, 10, 11, 12, 13, 16, 22, 23, 24, 25, 27
petrified wood 21, 29
Plateosaurus 10
Pompeii 8
Ranchero La Brea 19
resin, fossilized 5, 14, 15
Rocky Mountains 5
saber-toothed cats 19
sedimentary rock 5, 6, 11, 28
sharks' teeth 13
skeleton
    dinosaur 12, 14, 24
    giant sloth 23
    human 26, 27
    Irish elk 18
stromatolites 7
tar pits 19
Tiktaalik 22
Toba supervolcano 26
Tollund Man 18
tree bark 21
trilobites 7, 12
Tyrannosaurus rex 25
tyrannosaur 22
woolly mammoths 13, 16, 17
Yoho National Park 5